GW01007301

Other Mouse Village titles available:

Welcome to Mouse Village
Amanda Mouse and the Birthday Cake
Matt Mouse and the Big Surprise
Myrtle Mouse and the Naughty Twins

First published in Great Britain in 2000 by Madcap Books,
André Deutsch Ltd, 76 Dean Street, London, W1V 5HA

www.vci.co.uk

Copyright text © 2000 Gyles Brandreth/Madcap Books
Copyright illustrations © 2000 Mary Hall

The right of Gyles Brandreth and Mary Hall to be identified as the
author and illustrator of this work respectively has been asserted by them in
accordance with the Copyright, Designs and Patents Act, 1988

A catalogue record for this book is available from the British Library

Design by Traffika Publishing Ltd
Reprographics by Digicol Link

ISBN 0 233 99577 3

All rights reserved

Printed in Belgium by Proost nv

JACK MOUSE
AND THE
SCARECROW

by Gyles Brandreth
Illustrated by Mary Hall

MADCAP

Right at the edge of Mouse Village, you'll find a farm. It's called Jack's Farm. Can you guess why? Yes, that's right. It's called Jack's Farm because it belongs to Jack Mouse.

And here he is, picking cherries.

On his farm, Jack Mouse grows cherries, and strawberries, and raspberries, and apples, and pears, and carnations.

You can't eat carnations, of course. They're flowers. They look lovely and they smell nice. At least, that's what Jack Mouse thinks.

N ow you've met Jack Mouse, you must meet his helpers, Tom and Tim. They're twins.

Tom and Tim are town mice, and whenever they come to Mouse Village to stay at the Mouse Village Tea Shop with their Aunt Myrtle, they always visit Jack's Farm.

Today, the twins are out in the Big Field helping Jack Mouse to make a scarecrow.

'What's a scarecrow for?' asks Tim.

'To scare crows, of course!' says Tom.

'Not just crows,' adds Jack. 'We need the scarecrow to frighten *all* the birds, or they'll come and eat my cherries.'

At lunch time, Jack Mouse gives the twins a lift back into the village on one of his inventions. Jack's an inventor as well as a farmer.

Jack has invented a machine for washing windows, and another for picking flowers. Today, he's giving the twins a ride on his five-wheeled bicycle.

W hen they arrive at the Mouse Village Tea Shop, Myrtle Mouse is waiting for them. She's been out shopping and has bought herself a new hat.

'You look lovely!' says Jack Mouse.

'Thank you,' says Myrtle Mouse, twitching her whiskers.

'The twins have been helping me to make a scarecrow,' says Jack. 'Can they come back to the farm after lunch to help me finish it off?'

'Of course,' says Myrtle.

After lunch (it's cheese on toast - the twins' favourite), Myrtle Mouse has a little snooze and Tom and Tim do the washing-up.

'We've invented a washing-up machine,' says Tim.

'Aunt Myrtle will be pleased!' says Tom.

The washing-up done, the twins set off again for Jack's Farm. As they go, they see something in the hallway. They decide to take it with them. Can you guess what it is?

'That's right,' says Tom, 'It's Aunt Myrtle's new hat.'

'Does she know you've got it?' asks Jack Mouse.

'I'm sure she won't mind,' says Tim. 'It's just what our scarecrow needs, isn't it?'

'I suppose it is,' agrees Jack, scratching his head, 'And it does look lovely on him.'

You have to agree. The scarecrow looks very good indeed in Aunt Myrtle's brand new hat.

W hen it's time for tea, the twins walk home. They're happy mice. They feel that they've done a good day's work, and are surprised to find Aunt Myrtle looking so cross.

'What have you two been up to?' cries Myrtle Mouse. 'You naughty mice! My kitchen floor is covered with water and I can't find my beautiful new hat!'

'Sorry!' says Tim, 'We'll dry the floor.'

'Sorry!' says Tom, 'We'll find the hat.'

In the morning, bright and early, Tom and Tim and Myrtle Mouse make their way along the High Street, past the wishing well, and up Orchard Lane to Jack's Farm.

They find Jack Mouse and they find the scarecrow, but they don't find Aunt Myrtle's hat.

'Oh dear,' says Jack. 'It must have blown away.'

'Or been stolen by a crow,' says Myrtle Mouse, who is very cross indeed.

Myrtle and Jack and Tom and Tim look everywhere for that hat. They look high and low. They look round and about. They look in strawberry bushes and in beds of carnations. They can't see it anywhere. Can you?

'Yes!' shouts Tim, 'There it is!'

'It's on top of the chimney!' cries Tom.

'Oh dear,' sighs Myrtle Mouse.

'Don't worry,' says Jack. 'I've invented a machine for rescuing hats from chimneys.'

And he has.

'Up you go!' says Jack. And up the twins go. And down they come, bringing the hat with them.

'I'm surprised at how little damage there is,' says Aunt Myrtle, inspecting the hat. 'It's lost a cherry at the front, but it's got these nice black and white feathers instead.'

'It looks nicer than ever,' says Tim.

'This calls for a celebration,' says Jack. 'Let's have a bowl of strawberries and cream.'

'We'll pick them,' shout the twins.

'And if you don't mind,' says Myrtle Mouse, '*I'll* do the washing-up.'